The Westie Chronicles: Book One

The Tale of the Haunted Orchard

By V.G. Sims

Note to Reader: This is a work of fiction. The people, places or events in this narrative are a product of the author's imagination. Any resemblance to people, places or events in real life, past, present or future, are purely coincidental.

A portion of the author's proceeds of *The Tale of the Haunted Orchard* will be donated to the ASPCA.

Special thanks to Leonora Bulbeck for her outstanding editing skills and enthusiasm.

Special thanks to Ebooklaunch.com for their amazing cover art.

To my family: Bill, Will, Alana, and Dad

Thank you for your loving support and for listening to all my harebrained ideas in addition to the good ones.

To Gus, my inspiration and amazing friend. I think of you every day, still...

Table of Contents

CHAPTER ONE

AND SO, IT BEGINS ...

If you walk up Witch hill, which is steep and twisted all the way through, you will come to the top of an old apple orchard. It was once very beautiful, well cared for, full of life and loved as most beautiful things are; but the orchard has been sold to some not-so-nice people.

Now the trees grow wild and gnarled. Old apples lie rotting and abandoned by mice and people alike at their twisted bases and there are plenty of weeds to dig in to. It is very windy on top of the hill and you must walk past the forest of the million eyes. Past that there are two graveyards--one is for young heroes and a much older graveyard next to it is for old souls. There is a path from there that leads through the orchards and you can walk into the middle and look way out over the hill.

Don't go too far or you will come upon the old mad scientist's house. It lay abandoned for years, except for the rows of cages in the back. Stay clear of that. If you keep going, and finish the circle, you will come to my house. This is where our story begins. My family calls it the Westie Ranch.

I am the only Westie there right now, but that's the way I like it. Other dogs are so distracting--sniffing, scratching, growling, peeing on your stuff. I am the only one here who does that. I let the neighbors' dogs know it too--hooligans all.

The worst is that awful orange tabby cat from next door. He doesn't care. Every night at 4:30 in the morning, he comes to my house and pees on the doorstep. He knows I won't annihilate him because my family is sleeping and I need to keep them happy and safe. That's what Ethan would call an "opportunist." It's a good human word.

Ethan is my best friend. He takes me on walks and feeds me the most. He has some older folks who watch over him and I am responsible for them too; but I mostly hang out with him. We make a great team. He likes to be on the computer all day and half the night and it seems to annoy his parents a bit, but I don't mind. I like it when they are in the same room together and I can watch over them all.

In any case, our story starts on what seemed like any ordinary day. It was November, and the leaves were very bright because of the drought. Fiery colors--orange, yellows and reds framed the white fall sky. The outside animals were scurrying around trying to gather up stores for the coming cold days.

There was much buzz about whether the winter would be dry too. I think we were all hoping for snow.

I was hanging by a leaf pile eyeing some annoying chipmunks when Ethan came crashing out of the house. He had a new toy in his hand. He called it a "drone." He was always very excited about his drones and liked to tinker with them for hours on end. I don't mind because I like to sit at his feet by his workbench and wait for any crumbs that might drop from his snacks. I had just enough time to think about popcorn, one of my favorite snacks, when he came running past me, towards the orchard near our house.

"Gus, come on!" He called, running by me in a fury.

"*I'm on duty!*" I thought and raced to catch up.

We ran up the hill and through some tangled brush, across five rows of apple trees, into the center of one of the orchards. I had to dodge a bit as he kicked old apples in all directions.

Clonk! One landed right on my head but Ethan didn't notice. He was too excited. I was struggling to keep up. We were almost at the spot. There was a clearing where Ethan liked to fly some of his toys from. This drone was quite large, to me anyway. Its wires dangled precariously and it had an odd metallic smell. I tended to steer clear.

"It's got a camera on it!" said Ethan, excitedly. "Check this out Gus. I will be able to see all over the place, across the orchards and beyond. It even has night vision!"

I growled a little to show my hesitant approval. He took the control panel in both his hands and *ZIPPPP*! Up went his toy into the pale autumn sky. He had a phone dangling from around his neck. He would check it periodically and whoop it up. Ethan seemed pretty happy about it; and that made me happy.

"See," he said swapping hands to the control panel. I need to find a way to mount the screen on the control panel so I don't have to …"

Crash! There was a loud noise of collision as the drone nosedived from the sky. I craned my neck up and was just able to make out a large black shadow that dipped and cried out loudly. It made a wide circle in the air above us. I knew immediately: It was a hawk. Those birds were the bane of my existence. They flew above our yard, always trying to get at our chickens. This one was bigger than the scrawny hawks that I usually saw. I squinted at

10

the sky. It called again. I could just make out a tinkling of bells.

Then the creature circled and landed on the shoulder of a girl human about one hundred paces away from us. She looked over at us then began walking quickly to where we were. I bristled. I could make out her long scruffy hair under a floppy cap. She had on torn leggings and a canvas jacket.

"Hey! I am so sorry! Is your drone okay?" She stopped a few feet ahead of us.

"Yeah. I think so." Ethan looked down at the fallen beast. Wires and electronic appendages flopped haphazardly on the scratchy earth. He snapped a couple of pieces back together.

Why wasn't he mad at her? I thought. I would get yelled at for sure if I ate one of his toys. I moved in closer, unsure of how I was going to protect him.

"Is that your dog? He is super cute!" I watched her approach and stop a couple of feet in front of us. I blinked my eyes and could not believe it. She was carrying a hawk!

"I'm Eva and this is my bird, Vader." I eyed the beast reluctantly. Ethan smiled. The large predator sat comfortably on her forearm preening, gloating.

He was pretty amazing: Large and feathered, with a light head and large clawed feet. His eyes were gold and riveting and there were bells tied to his toes. He looked at me with suspicion. I held my ground. The girl had a big leather glove on. She tossed a cloth on her shoulder and he climbed up. Gently, she put a small hood over his head.

Harrumph, Ethan wouldn't dare do that to me … I mused, my confidence restored.

"I am Ethan O'Connor and this is Gus," he said, motioning me towards him. "Wow, that is some bird! Do you live around here?"

"Thanks! Yes, we just moved in." The wind whistled and she pushed a curl of golden hair behind her ear.

"Wow! Did you move next door to me? I am at 3 Cobblestone Lane."

"I am at 5! Yes, nice to meet you neighbor!" She leaned in to shake his hand.

"Err, do you go to Hamilton Middle School?" Ethan looked down at his feet and kicked an apple.

"Yes, I just transferred there last month. Seems okay so far but I don't know anyone yet."

"Yeah, it's okay. I can introduce you around … I never met anyone who had a hawk before!"

"Well, I never met anyone with a drone, so it's even!" She pulled a dead mouse out of a bag on her side and gave it to the hawk, who gobbled it in one bite.

Ethan's eyes widened but I could tell he was being his usual casual, cool self.

"I have got to head back and put him away. We hunted enough today."

"Would you like to come to my house and see my other drones? I probably got some cool footage of the crash."

"Yeah, that sounds great! Let me drop off Vader. I will meet you there in ten."

Ethan turned and headed back to the house. The bell of the old church in the town square tolled in the distance. We trod methodically between the rows of apple trees. I knew he was pleased because he was singing with his mouth closed as we went. I guess if Eva was his new friend, then she was mine as well. I wasn't too sure about that bird, but time would tell.

CHAPTER TWO

THERE IS SOMETHING GOING ON IN APPLEWOOD …

We ran up the stone steps, into the house, and Ethan slammed the door and hurriedly hung up his coat. The kitchen was warm with the pleasant smells of pea soup and apple crisp. His mother was cooking and called out to his dad upstairs. Ethan said hello and I rubbed my nose along the bottom of her corduroys. She looked down, smiled and passed me a little biscuit. I do love her. They were a great family. There was no time to linger that day though; there was business at hand.

"Ethan, Gus. Hi guys. Did you have fun in the orchards?" she said smiling.

"Hi Mom. Yes! Uh, and we met a new friend, Eva. She is our new neighbor. She is coming over for a bit."

"Well, that's great! I was hoping there were kids next door. There are cookies on the counter."

"Thanks Mom."

I took a sip of water while Ethan picked up a plateful of cookies, choc chip--off limits to me--from the counter. He circled back to the front door to let Eva in. I stopped behind him and peered at her from behind his legs. She looked smaller without her bird. Pumpkins and corn husks loomed on both sides of her on the front steps.

"Hi Eva. Come on in."

"Thanks," she said, grinning, and patted me on the head as she stepped into our house.

"Well, hello there." Miranda O'Connor, Ethan's mom, stepped out of the kitchen to greet Eva.

"Hello Mrs. O'Connor. I am Eva London. We recently moved next door."

"Well, welcome to the neighborhood. We are so happy to meet you. You are welcome here anytime. We will have to invite your folks over some night for supper."

Eva looked over at Ethan. "That would be great!"

"Come on Eva, let's go upstairs, I will show you the drones."

"It was nice meeting you," she called as they moved through the house and up the stairs.

A little red head popped out from behind a door in the bright green hallway. It was

Ethan's sister Tess. Her tangled mop of curls was as adorable as her toothless grin.

"Hi!" she called out. They were picking up speed and I struggled to get ahead of them.

"Hi there," called Eva over her shoulder. She peeked through some French doors at Ethan's dad working on a computer as they passed. "Does everyone in your family have such great red hair?"

"That's my little sister, Tess, and yes, I guess we do …have red hair I mean." he replied. Together they went up to the second floor and then climbed the flight of stairs behind the sliding bookcase to the attic room on the third floor.

"Wow! This place is amazing!" Eva spun in a small circle with her arms out. She was clearly impressed.

The attic room spanned the length of the house and was a very fun place to be. Cozy throw rugs and couches were strewn about. Colorful drawings and prints splashed across the beamed walls. Windows on both sides of the room showed two different scenes. One side showed the highway, which was one block over. Cars and trucks buzzed by. It was non-stop action. Conversely, on the opposite side of the room the windows looked out over acres of picturesque apple orchards, peacefully stretching out as far as the eye could see. It was quite dramatic, according to Ethan's mom. I just loved being up so high; it gave me perspective.

Westies don't have the longest legs. From the window seat, high up in the attic room, I could see so many of the woodland creatures that lived in the orchard below. Unfortunately, this included that evil neighbor cat. I could see its scrappy tail now, peeking out from under the hydrangea bushes next door, swishing its tail, twitching ...it was mesmerizing. *Devil*!

"Yeah, it's pretty cool up here." Ethan snatched me from my daydream. "No one bothers me," he said. "It's mostly off limits to my little sister, so my stuff doesn't get broken. Here are the drones and my computer. He motioned to a computer with three separate screens. "My dad helped me build this. It's pretty tricked out for gaming and stuff."

"Cool, I am not into games too much. I mean, I don't know that much about them. I like living things, animals. I am probably going to be a biologist someday. I don't know why I said that. But I love science and technology...err … I get it …" She plopped down in one to the comfy office chairs and swirled around.

"Yeah, technology is cool. Here, I can play back the crash." She leaned in to watch. Ethan punched a few keys and pulled up some images on the big screen. It was a playback of the hawk and the drone colliding. They watched it in slow motion several times, backwards and forwards. Both laughed when the drone collided with Vader, or vice versa. Feathers were flying everywhere.

"Oh no!"

"It's hard to tell whose fault it was!" Eva laughed. She grabbed a cookie from the plate. "I am glad neither Vader or your drone was hurt.

"Err, yes. I would call it a no-fault collision. No reason to raise rates," said Ethan.

Eva laughed and twirled her chair. She put her sneakered feet up on the sill of one of the long windows and looked down at the apple trees below, swaying gently in the afternoon breeze. Some black crows flew by the window oblivious to our presence.

"So, do you like living here in Applewood?" she asked.

"Yes, it's pretty cool. I like it a lot."

"I was wondering, have you noticed anything *strange* about the orchard?"

"Strange?" asked Ethan.

"Yes, odd." She dropped her tone and spoke softer. "I noticed it when I first moved in. There are a lot of lights in the sky and over the orchard at night. Sometimes I hear sounds like helicopters and low flying planes. When I look out, there is nothing there. Sometimes the air smells weird, like something's burning except I can't see any fires."

"Hmm," said Ethan looking serious.

"And there is that abandoned house in the middle of the orchard. I have seen lights there and in the graveyards as well but during the day it looks totally abandoned. I mean, who lives there? Who owns the orchards now?"

"Well, I have noticed those lights myself. It is pretty strange," he agreed.

Ethan went over to a bookcase and pulled out a large, thin book. He laid it down on the table. It had pictures of people dressed in clothes that looked like they were from the colonial days. The people looked very serious. They wore dark clothing and stared straight at the camera. The book had some old town maps in it as well.

"Here, this is where we live." He pointed to the center of one of the town maps. It was dotted with apple trees.

"Witch Hill?" gasped Eva.

"Yes. I have no idea why they called it that but it's pretty mysterious."

"The orchards have been here for over a hundred years. Most of the town was orchards and farmland."

"Wow, I bet it was beautiful," said Eva. She turned to look through the windows. Rows of apple trees sprawled across rolling hills as far as she could see. Houses dotted the edges. She saw a small church steeple in the distance. "It still is."

"And look, there was always this clearing in the middle, where that big house is now. There used to be a schoolhouse there I think. Then it burnt down in a fire and a huge house was built there in the late 1800s." He gestured to an old black and white picture of a big Victorian house with gables and trellises. The pointed roof pierced the clouds in the old black and white picture. Apple trees surrounded them and you could just make out one of the graveyards in the distance.

"Hmm, it looked old, even when it was new!" She ran a finger along the edge of the book.

"Yes, the local kids say a scientist moved in there and went crazy when most of his family died from the Spanish influenza. I think they took him away. The only one left was his youngest son. They say he was a scientist too and did all kinds of experiments on the animals that lived in this orchard. If you go close enough, you can see rows of cages in the back. But, I wouldn't go too close. He hasn't been seen in years but I am not altogether sure he is not still living in the house somewhere …I have seen lights too, inside the house and also moving around, trolling back and forth over the orchard at night. I have seen them around the graveyards too. And another thing …" He hesitated and pulled up a folder titled *Missing Pets*.

He opened it and pulled out a list of animals. There were several pictures of cats, dogs, and a *Missing* poster with an owl on it.

"I have been compiling a list. People's pets have been disappearing in the neighborhood. It's fairly recent, and troubling to say the least."

They both looked down at me. Ethan reached down and pet my head. Did they think I was going to be next? They were quiet for a minute.

Eva smiled. "I feel an adventure coming on!"

"Adventure?" Ethan zipped up his sweatshirt and pulled down his sleeves. "What do you have in mind?"

"Well, let's fly one of your drones at night, with a camera, over the orchard. I bet we can see what's going on," she said. "We can find out what the lights are and maybe even catch a glimpse of the mad scientist."

"Hmm." Ethan paused for a moment. He liked to think things through. "I guess we could do that. A couple of my drones have night vision; I can fly them in the dark -— for stealth missions. I even have a tiny camera we could fit on Vader for another perspective. If you guys are up to it."

"Yes. Let's do it!" Eva cried. "How about later tonight? It's still the beginning of the long weekend and all. The lights usually come later in the evening."

"Okay. Can you see the lights from your house? Text me when they come out and I will meet you outside your backyard. That way we can minimize our outside time. In case our folks get nervous. What's your cell? Here is mine."

Got it thanks ☺. Eva texted.

"Well, I guess I will see you later!" She got up and made her way to the door. I heard her feet clomping down the stairs. I looked over at Ethan. He was lost in thought, planning something no doubt.

I hopped up to the window and looked out over the apple trees. They swayed gently in the breeze. Several rows on one side had been cut down. Gnarled branches and weeds lay in piles, ready to be burned no doubt. I dropped my gaze and peered down into Eva's backyard. I saw her run across the yard and disappear into the back porch. I scanned the hydrangeas. The cat was gone. Things were about to get interesting.

CHAPTER THREE

A MOONLIT NIGHT COMES TO AN END

That night the golden autumn moon was almost full. It was windy and the leaves crunched underfoot as Ethan and I made our way as quietly as we could through the back path leading to Eva's house. I could make out some orange lights up in the sky, circling and moving through the clouds in a grid like pattern across the darkness.

We walked uphill along the edge of the orchard to get to Eva's house. Being a Westie, and good at my job, it was hard to stay focused with the many eyes of the night creatures upon us as we made our way up the path and through the woods. Their eyes shone brightly from all around the woodland path. A desperate chipmunk darted across the path and grabbed an acorn. I had more important things to do than chase after him.

A large black crow sat on the top of Eva's house. It was devouring some small animals that looked like mice or maybe small bats. I could see their desperate movements in the night shadows. Ethan didn't notice.

It sure was spooky out that first night of our adventure. I had a sense of foreboding. That is, I felt like something was about to happen. The same way your mouth waters a bit when one of your owners brings out a treat. You think you may be getting it but not quite sure either.

Ethan sent her a text and we sat down on the ground to wait. The moon shone brightly through the clouds. A solitary owl hooted in the distance.

"Hello!"

We both jumped. Eva had come up behind us in the brush.

"Sorry, I wanted to get something from the shed first." She reached up and put the very large bird on her shoulder. He looked bigger and somehow less friendly than before. "Vader loves to hunt at night, although usually not this late." She shrugged and he took off, flew up, and landed on Eva's roof. It was a colonial house like ours--a new house that looked old. He swooped down and effortlessly took away whatever bounty the large crow had been eating.

"Reeakk!" The crow called out mournfully and flew into the trees. It knew it had been beaten. Vader remained a minute on the roof, eating his prey. The moonlight shone on his eyes. He turned his silver head, which acted like a spotlight, and gazed at us. One thing was for sure: That bird had charisma. He swooped down noiselessly and landed on Eva's forearm.

"Wow," said Ethan. "That is quite a bird!"

"Yeah, he is very strong, and a good friend too! Okay, let's go."

We all agreed and walked the few remaining yards to the orchard. We stopped at the no trespassing sign. It had fallen into the weeds. Ethan paused to read it. "No hunting or trespassing at any times. Violators will be prosecuted. Courtesy of Doughton Properties, LLC." He propped it back up. "Those are the guys that bought the orchards. We are waiting to see what they are going to do but it doesn't look good. I heard they were going to cut all the orchards down and put in an outlet mall."

"That's pretty horrible. I mean, what is going to happen to all the animals that live here?" said Eva.

I had heard Ethan's folks talking about it at dinner one night. I remembered the worry in their voices. They were afraid the developers would take our house. I remember thinking at the time about all the animals that would have to move too. Some were surely too little or old and frail to make it. I would show those developers what's what if I ever got within close enough range.

I hopped over the brush and followed my friends. They said the builders were even planning to bring the highway closer. I heard a truck rumble. An owl hooted in the distance. I could make out the shadows of the old graveyard in the background. I knew there was a family of turkeys hiding behind the stones. I looked up and saw one sitting in a pine tree above us as we walked by. It blinked a big googly eye at me. I didn't say anything though, poor things. They weren't the brightest creatures and it was almost turkey season. I was grateful I had a house to live in and a family who loved me. We walked along quietly and stopped before the clearing. The air smelled crisp and cool, like fall and apples, and wood smoke.

"Let's set up here," said Ethan. He knelt and unpacked some equipment.

"Okay, can I help with anything?" Eva asked.

"No thanks, it will just take a sec," he said, and unwrapped two of his drones from a canvas bag. "I think I will fly two tonight and get footage from the orchard and over the scientist's house. I am going to attach the small drone camera to Vader's foot. It has night vision and video capabilities. That should give us a totally different perspective. Also, I won't have to control two at the same time."

"Sounds good. You can attach it here, by the bells." She gently turned Vader's talon. "That tells me where he is, in case I lose him on a hunt." She turned and pointed up at the sky. "That's where I saw the lights about a half hour ago. They were near the top of the orchard, almost to the old church."

Together we scanned the night sky. There was a faint sulfuric smell in the air. Suddenly, a plane flew overhead, casting an orange glow from its lights and leaving behind a trail of white smoke. The smoke streamed and expanded into the cool air.

I am not sure about Ethan and Eva, but I felt dizzy, all of a sudden. My feet were tingling. It was the strangest feeling. My head felt light, like it was floating above my body. For a moment, my vision blurred. I shook my head from side to side.

What was happening to me? I thought.

"Are you okay, old man?" Ethan said looking down at me. I must have stumbled a bit but I gave him a short growl, to let him know not to baby me.

"Okay, let's get these birds in flight!"

"Right," whispered Eva and threw up her arm. Both bird and drone went up into the night sky.

As if on cue, some lights appeared from behind the church square. A plane emerged, flying low on the horizon. Pale orange lights shone from the control panels but it was otherwise black. It flew past the orchards and into the surrounding neighborhoods and then back up, forming a linear pattern. Pale white lines faded into the clouds on the horizon. The plane turned and headed our way. Ethan's drone was still close to us but Vader had flown over the old mansion.

The last thing I remember was the plane flying overhead and their voices sounding far away and muffled.

I awoke in the attic room. Ethan's face was very close to mine. He must have carried me back home. My head was swimming. I jumped out of his arms and off the couch. Shakily I stood up.

"Gus! You're back! You had me scared. Here, drink some water!" He pushed my water dish at me. I took a sip listlessly. Daylight hit me like the jerk of a choke collar. I winced. The sun was just beginning to rise on the eastern edge of the orchard. It was starting to stream freely in through the windows and making my head ache. "Easy now!" he said looking concerned

I looked around. Where was Eva and Vader? She came around the couch and pet me on the head.

"I think he will be alright. Poor Gus. You are safe now!" She pet me warmly and scratched my ears. "I love how he has one ear that goes up and the other down. So, what is going on? Do you have Vader's footage? It's not like him to not come back right away when I call."

"Hopefully this sheds some light on the subject. This is the footage from the camera on his foot," he said.

Ethan sat down next to me on the couch. We all stared up at the screen. Together, we watched Vader take off into the night from his perspective. Flying up into the clouds, the edges of his wings were visible. We could see out over the orchards from Vader's point of view. He turned back and we could see ourselves crouching on the edge of the orchard. Ethan sent a drone off in the direction of the planes and the hawk continued forward and banked left into the middle of the orchard. He approached the house. There was a light flickering in the second story window. It looked like perhaps a candle. A plane flew overhead and left a gray cloud that drifted down, covering the camera's lens.

Suddenly, Vader seemed to be losing altitude. The house rose up and the next thing we saw was the underside of an old porch railing. The door opened slowly and a person stepped out.

Eva drew in an audible breath. We all froze. The camera stopped at a man's knees but when he bent down to pick up Vader, we caught a glimpse of his dark almond shaped eyes and a handlebar moustache. Like the kind in that French detective series Ethan's mom and I like to watch on Sundays. He looked at the camera for a second. I felt like he could see us.

"Who is that?" whispered Ethan.

"Is Vader okay?" There were tears in Eva's eyes. Ethan reached over and squeezed her hand. I put my head on her ankle. Their eyes were glued to the screen.

The man looked at the camera then pulled off the bells. The last thing we saw was a shot of the sky and the big harvest moon and then blackness.

"He must have tossed the camera away! We have to go back!"

"Did he do something to hurt Vader? The same thing that made Gus pass out?" Eva jumped off the couch.

"I am not sure. Wait. Let's look at the footage from the drone," said Ethan. With the click of the button we were seeing the orchard from a different view.

I sat back on the couch and watched the huge screen. The planes came swooping in. From above, I saw myself fall into the weeds and Ethan stop to pick me up. My paws dangled below his hands and he pulled me to his chest. He had the most horrified look on his face. My heart twinged. Vader took off over the house and then nosedived into some old rosebushes next to the scientist's porch. The clouds from the plane descended around us.

"Hey," said Eva. "I don't think the guy in the house hurt Vader. It was those guys in the plane. What were they spraying?"

"No idea, but it hurt our pets for sure." He knelt, and gave me a piece of popcorn. I took it as usual. "I think Gus is okay but what they did has to be illegal, and unsafe."

"Well, we have to go back and get Vader. How do we protect ourselves from the fog?"

"I have these!" He went to a cabinet and pulled out two gas masks. Eva raised her eyebrows.

"What can I say? I like to collect equipment." He looked down at Gus.

"Sorry buddy, you are staying here--at least until we figure out what's going on." He reached over and scratched my neck. "I don't know what I would do if something happened to you."

"Should we tell your folks?" Eva went over to the windowsill and peered down at the yard, just as Ethan's mom and Tess got in the car to go on errands. I knew his dad had left to go on his weekend jog--that could take a while.

I shook my head. "It's daytime now. I will text to tell them where we are going. Let's head on over and ask for Vader. I will keep my camera on for security. There is one for you too," he said, motioning to Eva.

"Gus, you can man the couch and watch the video. Run down and grab the folks if anything goes wrong!"

I looked up at him and nodded my shaky head. Nothing would stop me.

CHAPTER FOUR

THE PROFESSOR'S LAIR

I watched from home on the big screen as the two friends approached the old gray house and knocked loudly on the door. They both had gas masks on and looked fairly odd, to say the least, like big walking bugs. Ethan pulled off his mask. He was in rare form; I had never seen him look so determined. I wished I could be there to protect them both. No one answered. He knocked again and tried the old copper doorknob. It creaked open. He looked over at Eva. She had on a little camera too and I could see her point of view on the bottom right of my screen. She reached past him and opened the door.

With a bang, it flew open. Eva walked right in, grabbing Ethan's hand behind her. With trepidation, Ethan followed her into the house. It was poorly lit and it looked old and dusty. Old brown furniture and boxes littered the room. Old drapes with tears and stains covered the windows. It looked unlived in and unwelcoming. A thick layer of dust covered everything. Eva pulled off her mask.

"It looks like no one has lived here in years." She wrinkled her nose. "Smells musty."

"Hello!" Ethan called. The house seemed dark, with old clothes draped across furniture that was strewn about in a haphazard way. They walked past an old staircase. A light shone from under a door built in to it.

"Down there!" she said pointing at the door. He reached ahead and tested the knob, turning it softly to and fro. It was open. He looked at Eva. She nodded. Slowly he turned it again and opened the door

Immediately, they were bathed in light. Ethan and Eva squinted and looked down a long hallway. The floor sloped downward gradually then turned a corner. They hesitated. There was no telling what or who they would find or how much danger they were in.

"Let's go!" said Eva. "Vader could be in trouble."

Ethan nodded and they proceeded.

Their faces gleamed with amazement by what they saw. There was bright light shining all around them. It was like being outside on a sunny day. The walls had life-sized images of the orchards projected somehow onto them. This was in huge contrast from the creepy interior of the house. Ethan blinked his eyes and looked up at the ceiling. But there was none. Above them, blue sky and fluffy clouds floated by.

"What is this?" he exclaimed. "Do you feel the breeze? It even smells like the orchard down here."

Suddenly the pictures on the walls changed. There were pictures of all of us, running through the orchards, with me and Vader before we got separated. This was followed by pictures of Eva and Ethan running to the front door. Then they were walking through a tunnel, with videos of themselves on the walls. It made my head spin to watch.

"This is creepy!" exclaimed Eva, craning her head back and forth as she moved.

"Raaaark!"

It was the bird!

"Vader! I hear him!" she cried.

They ran down the incline and around a corner to find themselves in a huge room. They must have been underground, under the old house. The room was quite long and covered on both sides with shelves and shelves of books and beautiful oil paintings. There were two long tables with laboratory equipment on them. The "windows" were projections of the orchard that reached up to the soaring copper ceiling. It was amazing. There was a long wooden table and workbench and a leather chair facing a roaring fireplace. There was a large man in the chair, facing the fire, and on the back of the chair was the bird.

"Vader!" cried Eva. She ran ahead. In one swift motion the hawk turned and flew to her shoulder. He looked into her eyes and chirped, clearly happy to see her. She hugged him and sighed. It was wonderful.

Ethan moved ahead. "Who are you? And what did you do to our pets?"

"Ethan!" exclaimed Eva.

"I should be asking you that, *Ethan,* except I already know." The man got up from the chair and slowly turned around. He was tall, and old. He had wrinkles around his eyes, which twinkled with amusement and a small curled mustache, which quivered when he spoke.

"You are Ethan O'Connor. You live with your mom, dad, sister Tess, dog Gus, and an odd assortment of chickens at 3 Cobblestone Lane. You have a penchant for drones and all things electronic." He turned to Eva and smiled. "You are Eva London. Having recently moved here with your folks, your beautiful hawk and a very large, somewhat disagreeable cat, you live next door to Ethan. I have seen you both wandering around in my orchards. Err, but really, I don't mind."

"I heard you sold them," said Eva, moving closer to him with her beloved bird back on her shoulder

"Well, I did sell many acres unfortunately. I was trying to find a way to pay off the taxes and buy back some more of the land when some big shots moved in and bought it overnight. Now I just have this one acre of land in the middle. But they are trying to get that from me as well."

Ethan eyed him with distrust and scanned the room. His eyes fell on the workbench littered with gadgets and electronics.

"I didn't hurt your animals, by the way. *They* did. They dropped some kind of tranquilizer from the air. From my calculations, they have been doing it for months. It's dangerous for the wildlife and highly illegal. If no one acts, they will do a lot worse than make our house pets groggy.

"Hoo hoo hoot!" They both jumped. There was a large gray owl sitting on one of the old bookcases. They hadn't even noticed. It blinked its gigantic golden eyes at them then turned its head unnaturally around.

"Yes, that's Herodotus. I also call him H." He looked over at Vader. "I am a sucker for birds of prey."

Eva walked forward and shook the man's hand. "Well, thank you for helping my bird. I am sorry for coming into your house without being invited."

"You are welcome. I don't have many visitors, but I am glad to meet you." Ethan felt something run across his foot and looked down. A rust colored woodchuck the size of Eva's cat scurried across the room and jumped onto the leather chair.

"Ah yes, that is Ari. He lives here with me as well. I am a biologist. I like to rehabilitate some of the orchard animals that need my help before I set them free again. Ari was curious about everything here and refused to go back to the wild. The orchard isn't as hospitable as it used to be. Many of his friends aren't making it lately I am afraid. With the clearing of the land there is less food and water for them. Their ecosystem has been disrupted." He gazed out the projected windows. A helicopter fly by in the distance.

The children looked up in time to see a small group of barn swallows fly across the ceiling. A huge fish tank bubbled in the corner. A creature resembling an octopus scurried behind an amazing chunk of white coral. The place was teaming with life.

"And your name is?" queried Eva

"Professor Winter Maddock, PhD," read Ethan out loud off a framed diploma perched precariously on a bookshelf.

"You can call me W for short," said the professor, agreeably.

"Or Professor W," said Eva smiling.

"Stay for lunch and I will fill you in on the goings on around here. I am at a quandary. That is, I really don't know what to do."

"Well, we can't stay long. I want to check on Gus. He was still a little out of sorts when we left."

"Of course," said the professor. "Here is your drone by the way." He also handed back the small camera that had been tied to Vader's foot.

"Thanks!" said Ethan. In all the excitement, he had forgotten about his equipment.

"I made a little modification to it. Hope you don't mind. It now has a homing beacon, so you can find it if it gets lost again."

"Wow! Thanks," said Ethan smiling. "Err, maybe we could stay a bit longer. I would like to know what is going on around here."

"Yes," interjected Eva. "We have been noticing strange lights at night in the orchards, and many of the pets and orchard animals have been disappearing. I was wondering what was happening to them."

"It's not just a question of what, but of *who*," said the professor opening up two local newspapers. Englebert Kettlebum and his right-hand man Pierre LeFue. Owner and chief planner of Doughton Enterprises, LLC leered up at them from the tattered pages.

"Who are those guys?" asked Eva, coming in for a closer look.

"Those are the ones who bought the orchards. They told the town they were going to put up some nice senior centers, a whole retirement community with golf courses and community centers. The town okayed their plans, but they have other designs for the land." He tossed another paper down on the table.

In the picture, Kettlebum was shaking hands with an equally creepy looking man. He had small rounded teeth and a big rounded head. His pants were hanging low. It was amazing that gravity did not finish them off. LeFue frowned in the shadows of the photo. His black ponytail was streaked with white and slicked back from his equally shiny and impossibly high forehead. He had beady looking eyes and his skinny hairless arms fell away from his biker shirt which had an illuminati symbol in the middle of it. He looked angry and hungry. Kettlebum looked like he had eaten too much but could probably eat more. He was grinning like the Cheshire Cat.

"I have read about them," said Ethan. "What's their plan?"

"I believe it's this." Professor W. leaned in and put a tablet next to Ethan.

"Tower Industries Pipeline Project?"

"Yes. Fossil fuels are the energy of the past and now unfortunately, the future for Applewood anyway."

"A pipeline right through the orchards and our neighborhood? No way!" cried Eva.

"Way," Ethan gasped as he scanned through the company's projected project.

"But pipelines always fail. It's dirty energy. What would happen if it leaked into the orchard? I thought the town was committed to green energy?"

"That's a ruse, just like Kettlebum's building plans. Everything about these guys is Crooked," said the professor.

"Here, see, they changed the town government rules about building developments, then took a payoff and paved the way for unethical folks to come in and profit. They are planning on taking a bunch of the surrounding houses under 'eminent domain' laws. Unfortunately, that is your house, my house and most of the surrounding neighborhood."

"How awful! I love it here. What a huge loss," exclaimed Ethan.

"To us and all the animals," said Eva looking out at the projected orchard. Then down at the black crosses on the tablet, marking out their houses. "It's such a great place to live. There is so much life here. I wish there was a way to fix this."

"Well, there is always room for change when something hasn't happened yet," suggested the professor. "The key is taking immediate action."

Eva turned and walked to the fireplace. There were multiple framed pictures and works of art. One older painting depicted a tall and striking Indian chief standing on a cliff. He was clothed in buckskin and his headdress was large and colorful. His powerful arms were raised to the sky and storm clouds rained down on the valley below.

"Who is that?" she said.

"Why, that is Chief Passaconaway. He was a powerful Native American chief and ruled the lands from the lower valley up to the white mountains. He was a great warrior and sorcerer, before we took his lands that is. It is said he could control the weather and call up fire as well as storms. He had lands in the area and enjoyed hunting here, close to Witch Hill. He tried to warn his people of the settlers' greed but they outsmarted the natives and took their land."

"So interesting," she mused. "I love hearing about the people that came before us."

"Yes, it seems he had some control over the weather. There's some folk stories that report he called up bursts of powerful winds and thunderstorms to stop some minor skirmishes in the area," said the professor. "He ultimately lost to the settlers, but his fight was one against many."

"Hmm," murmured Ethan. He rotated the drone in his hands and looked up at the clouds. "Maybe we could try our hand at that before the *two* become many …"

"The clouds and the planes …" said Eva. "They dropped chemicals into the clouds. That's how they tranquilized our animals. That is so harsh! What will they do to us?"

"They are trying to control us," remarked the Professor. "They don't care how they do it. Kettlebum and LeFue need the town's approval to take control of the orchard land and put in their pipeline. I think they are planning on poisoning the whole town with that stuff to make the people more compliant, more ready to sign the papers. I think they are interested in fast profits and moving on, with none of the safety protocols in place to protect the community, the environment or the animals."

"What if *we* controlled the weather?" Said Ethan.

"What?" both the professor and Eva said simultaneously.

"Professor, how do we get our hands on one hundred gallons of soap suds? I think I am getting a plan."

CHAPTER FIVE

A VILLAIN APPEARS

Bang! Bang! Bang!

"What's that?" asked Eva. Again, a loud knocking was sounded.

The professor walked over and waved his hand over a ceramic chimpanzee figurine sitting on one of the bookcases. Suddenly, the orchard window scenes changed to pictures of his front and back doors. There he was, LeFue in all his glory, rapping on the front door. He narrowed his eyes and squinted down to a flier in his hand. He pulled out his cell.

"Yeah, Bert, I know. He isn't home. No, he will leave. We will make him an offer he can't refuse. Heh heh." With a sneer, he kicked his

German Shepherd. The poor creature was sitting on the steps sniffing the door. It yelped and ran down across the yard.

"What a creep," growled Eva. Vader lifted his wings and shook. The woodchuck dove under the couch. LeFue leaned in to the camera and looked inside the house. His greasy forehead squeaked against the glass. "Yah, no, we will get him out, don't worry. Until tonight!" He took a large wad of pink slimy gum out of his mouth and stuck the flier to the window blocking the camera. Professor W. pushed a button and caught him from the other angle.

"Come on Adolf," he called to the dog which scurried over and skulked along behind him. With a flurry of expletives, he hopped on his four-wheeler and did several donuts around the house, kicking up dirt and leaving a trail of dust and flailing birds behind as he plowed through a small group of starlings. He cackled and peeled away. The dog ran behind after him. The two grew smaller and smaller on the screen like a spitball disappearing into the distance.

The professor, punched a computer and called up a close up picture of the flier, stuck to the window.

Applewood Town Meeting:

Where: The High School Fields

When: Immediately following the Turkey Bowl Celebration

Agenda: The building of your new Senior Center and Recreational area.

Congratulations to all!

All those attending will be entered in our raffle

Win a huge $50,000!!!

All your questions will be answered

We value your input!

Doughton Industries, LLC.

"What are they up to?" asked Eva.

"That is most likely where they can get a large amount of people together at one time. If I were a betting man, I would bet they are planning on dropping the tranquilizers at the Turkey Bowl, over the football fields and bleachers," mused Professor W. He clicked the screen and brought the orchards back to life on the windows. The owl took flight and flew above their heads, landing on a large tree in a pot by the fireplace.

"The whole town will be there!" exclaimed Ethan. "My mom enters the apple pie contest every year! My dad tries every year for the biggest giant pumpkin, Although this year, not so much. I think there has been a cat digging around in our pumpkin patch."

Eva drew in her breath and turned pink.

"Anyway, most of the town will be there in one concentrated spot. After the football game they will be voting on the building permits Phase One," continued the Professor, "So ..."

"So ... it's the perfect opportunity to get the whole town in one place and drop tranquilizers on them. If everyone is feeling dazed, they will be more apt to vote yes on the building agenda. What a dastardly plan," wailed Eva. "We have to take action and change this! Expose those villains!"

"We need to get the town to listen to us to do that," said Ethan. "We need to use Kettlebum and LeFue's voices against them. That way we would not be the only ones speaking. That's it! I will sneak into their office and video them talking about their plans."

"How do you know they are going to talk about it?" Eva asked.

"My dad was a businessman for a while, and I learned from his stories. People with puffed up egos love to talk about themselves. I will tape their conversation then play it back over the widescreen at the Turkey Bowl. That will get everyone's attention. Kenny from school is my friend and the middle school band manager. He can let me into the control room after the game. We will get footage of them putting what they think are tranquilizers onto the plane. We just have to switch the chemicals out first, so no one gets hurt.

"Hopefully, the professor can help us with that ..." Eva turned to the professor.

He nodded with a sparkle in his eye. "I would be happy to oblige."

"And hopefully Eva can cause a big enough distraction first, so the professor can get onboard. With a little luck, that pipeline is going to be a pipe dream!"

"It will!" cried Eva, "I have a good feeling about this!"

CHAPTER SIX

VADER AND I CAUSE A STIR

The following Saturday at precisely 11:00 a.m., two hours before the Turkey Bowl game was starting, Eva and the professor walked slowly to the old warehouse on the edge of the apple orchard. Their heads bent close together and they spoke quietly. Their tone sounded very serious.

The orchard sat about a quarter of a mile from the open air stadium, where the football game was getting ready to start. I could hear the high school band tuning up in the distance. I sniffed the cool autumn air. I walked slightly ahead, casing the place out. My white paws crunched through drying out leaves and prickly weeds. I could smell, apples, diesel fuel and further away, but unmistakably, popcorn. I shook my head.

"Focus!" I told myself. "My friends need me!"

"You are sure they keep the plane here?" I heard Eva ask. She pulled the velvet hood down tighter over Vader's head. He shifted his weight and jingled a bell with one of his talons.

"Yes, I have been gathering footage on these guys for a while," replied Professor W. "If you can distract them, I can slip onto the plane, plant a camera for more proof and swap out the tranquilizers for something more …fun." He patted a big canvas knapsack and swung it onto his shoulder.

"I …I just can't thank you enough for coming out here and helping me," he said.

Eva smiled warmly. "We are helping each other. It's everyone's orchard. Especially the animals. I don't want to see it chopped down, and I don't want to have to move again. We will fix this, you will see." She narrowed her eyes and whispered. "Here comes someone." The professor backed towards the entrance to the warehouse and pretended to tie his shoe. Eva stepped forward as a pale man in overalls approached.

"Hey, there," she called.

"Hey." He walked towards her with a quizzical look on his face.

"I am on the Hamilton school newspaper team. I am writing a story about small engines. Englebert Kettlebum, my uncle, said I could come out and check out the plane. I have an interest in things that fly."

Eva stared him straight in the eyes as she unhooked Vader's hood. There was no hesitation in her movements.

"I don't know about that."

"Stop! Who are you?"

Suddenly a man sprang at her from around the corner. He seemed to pop out at them like a child playing a prank. A nightmare in black spandex, his greasy black and white ponytail stuck out the back of a mirrored bike helmet. Eva would recognize that creepy man anywhere. It was LeFue. He had a road bike with him and threw it down on the ground perilously close to her feet. Eva jumped.

"Why I'm, I'm…" Eva began.

"Raaaark!" With a subtle sweep of her arm, Vader took off and flew at LeFue. He ducked and Vader swooped back at the two men. Artfully the great bird swung around and poked the mechanic in his eye with a wing tip. LeFue ducked and ran back behind the building. Vader followed.

"What? Hey! My eye! I'll sue you!"
LeFue yelled and ducked again, his head down,
giving the professor just enough time to slip
into the warehouse. Quietly the professor shut
the door.

In a cloud of fury, LeFue hopped on his
ATV and came barreling back to the front of
the building. His German Shepherd ran behind,
snarling.

"Get out of here!" he shrieked, skidded
to a stop and revved his engines. "What is your
name?"

"Why, I'm so sorry. He never …" Eva
stumbled.

"Hey!"

Vader swooped and dove at them again.

I scooted in after the professor. I looked
back to see a cloud of feathers spun into a cloud

of dust. I could just make out Eva causing a ruckus and apologizing to the men at the same time. She was great! Our plan was working. We were in!

I trotted beside Professor W. with a camera safely secured to my favorite collar. I scanned the area. The warehouse was big and dark, with towering steel ceilings. The powdery dirt floor was getting my paws filthy but we trudged on.

The plane was in the middle of the warehouse, facing outwards. Its nose pointed towards some big glass covered doors. Filtered light streamed onto the plane. The place smelled of gasoline and dirt.

Quickly and quietly we crept up to the aircraft.

"Stay here and bark if anyone comes," the professor whispered. He twirled his moustache and adjusted his glasses. He looked nervous but determined.

I was glad to be part of the plan. The professor walked up the steel airplane steps. I could see several drums inside the plane when he opened the metal door and stepped in.

That must be where the chemicals were, the stuff that made me feel woozy, I thought.

We were going to get these guys, I knew it. Minutes passed, I looked around the warehouse. There were some barrels marked "do not open" strewn about by the walls. I sure hoped the professor would be able to get to the barrels inside.

Suddenly I heard footsteps approaching. I ducked behind the airplane stairs. Two men stood smoking by the entrance. One of them approached the plane. Now it was time for my distraction.

"Bark! Bark! Bark!" I called out loudly. With remarkable dexterity, I circled the two men approaching the plane. I swung my head around. I could see the professor crack open the door. I saw LeFue come in the front door, bellowing to the mechanics. I had to lead them away now.

"Hey you!" he yelled.

"Bark! Bark!" I nipped at the shorter one's heels. He made a move to grab my collar and I dodged backwards and nipped the other one on the butt.

"Yow!" He cried out and jumped about three feet into the air. "What is it with this place? Are all the animals crazy?"

I ran between the other one's legs and led them towards a side door.

"Well they are all going to be sleeping soon. Aren't you boy? Nice doggy. Come here so I can …" LeFue moved towards me and lifted up a large wrench.

I wasn't afraid. I let him get close to me while, from the corner of my eye, I spied the professor, climbing out of the plane and slipping out the door he came in. He did it! Now it was time for my exit. I circled around and picked up the mechanic's hat.

"Hey!" He bolted after me, but who was chasing who?

I led them towards the side door that Eva had left slightly ajar for me earlier. I dropped the hat in a pile of stinky garbage and ran outside with time to spare. They were no match for my Westie speed! I bolted across the street (after looking both ways) and met up with Eva behind a group of apple trees.

"Gus!" Eva called, kneeling on the patchy grass to pat my ears and shrug my shoulders. Vader was perched on her shoulder, looking quite proud of himself.

"What a good dog! So far, we are doing great. I see the professor heading our way!"

"Plan A accomplished!" she said, smiling.

"Yes," said Professor W. He was out of breath but smiling and looked both flustered and relieved. "I was able to neutralize the tranquilizer and plant a camera. Now, all we have to do, is sit back, and watch the show! Let's get back to the house. We can watch how Ethan is doing from the safety of the lab."

"Yes. I wonder how he is doing," said Eva. "Great work Gus!"

That was enough for me. My work with them was done. I barked once and took off across the field in search of my best friend. It was easy to pick up Ethan's scent. On to Plan B

…

CHAPTER SEVEN

A STEALTHY MISSION

Ethan walked quickly through the field, kicking apples as he went. He was lost in thought. I was wondering myself how he was going to get into their office and how he would get them to talk. He looked relieved to see me.

"Hey old man," He reached down to pet me and adjusted my monitor. "Am I glad to see you! We've got to be stealthy but I am sure we can get this done. The truth will prevail." He stood up and looked toward the stadium. "I know where their office is. Follow me!"

We weaved through the people. The whole town was there to celebrate the Turkey Bowl. Families and teenagers, older folks and little ones. Everyone looked happy and busy.

And, there was lots of food to be had. They kept dropping bits of half-eaten caramel apples, hot dogs and popcorn! It was tough to stay focused. We approached a tall glass covered building set on top of the bleachers.

"This is it, I am pretty sure," he said under his breath. We climbed to the top. "Kenny told me their office is in there. Look, you can see the whole town from up here. All the bigwigs are gathering."

He pointed to a group of men talking a few bleachers down. Kettlebum was right in the middle, his face red and round. He laughed loudly and smoked a big cigar, his pants hung low on his hips. The others hung on his words like seagulls waiting for a snack. LeFue was to his left, talking into his Bluetooth and snickering. He grabbed some popcorn from a little girl next to him when no one was looking. I narrowed my eyes.

"Come on, we can get in and plant our cameras in their office. He pulled out a few paper bags from his knapsack. They said "Orchard Catering" on the side.

"If anyone asks, we are dropping off their lunch. He unzipped his jacket and had a green Orchard Café T-shirt decal. "Do you like it? I made it with our printer. Here is one for you boy." He knelt down and put a doggy T-shirt on me with the same wording. I didn't mind. Honestly, I look good in that color.

"Okay, let's go!" Ethan ran up a small set of stairs and checked a few doors in the hallway. "This is it," he whispered. He opened a door leading into a dark office with an expensive looking desk and chairs. Large windows looked out over the stadium. A fish tank with a black eel in it bubbled in the corner. There was a bar off to one side. I decided to check it out. I smelled corn chips.

Ethan sat down at the desk and began typing on the keyboard. He was looking for evidence. "Nothing too important here …except …" Ethan reached under the desk and pulled out the computer stand. There were papers stuck there. "Bingo! This is an agreement with the Tower Industries Pipeline Project corporation. Here is a map showing the pipeline going right through the orchard." He snapped some pictures with his phone. "Hope you get this at home Professor! Now, all we need is a confession. I am putting the camera in the light fixture above the desk. Just one more for better sound …" Ethan climbed up onto the desk and was reaching for the light when …

"Hey kid! What are you doing?" LeFue burst in out of nowhere, eyes bulging, teeth glaring. He whipped his ponytail around and sweat went flying across the room. I scrunched down behind the bar.

"Umm, Orchard Catering ..."

"Get out, we didn't order any food. What are you doing up there? What's in your hands?"

"N-Nothing!" stammered Ethan.

LeFue narrowed his eyes and pulled out a tiny gun. It looked like a toy. "Give me that! Whatever it is in your hand and get out!"

Warily, Ethan stepped forward and handed him his camera. I growled softly. He brought his hand to his lips and signaled me to cool it. I crouched behind the bar. LeFue couldn't see me. I was fuming. That villain actually pulled a gun on my best friend.

"Yeah, that's it," he said. "Get out of here before I call the cops!"

Ethan slunk slowly from the room. As he opened the door he made a stay motion with his hand behind his back, before LeFue shoved him rudely out into the hallway and slammed the door. I still had my camera. The whole thing was now up to me.

"Amateurs," growled LeFue. "I should have popped him." He put down the tiny gun and held up the camera and twisted it about in his hands. He picked up a heavy pencil sharpener and bashed it on the desk. Pieces scattered everywhere. "That will show them. We will round up all these peasants. Stupid people in their stupid houses. They will rue the day they ever heard of …"

The door slammed open again. The sound and smell of farts and cigar smoke filled the air. I changed my position to find a better viewing point. It was Kettlebum in all his stinky glory.

"Well, LeFue. How is it going." He belched and took a huge puff from his cigar. A chunky gold ring made mirrored snowflakes on the ceiling. "Any *glitches*?"

"None whatsoever. These peasants will never know what hit them. I see you had the town council eating from your fingers," sneered Lefue.

"Yes, heh heh heh," agreed Kettlebum, holding up a grimy finger and smiling at the memory. "They are like putty." He spat a piece of his stinky cigar, dripping with saliva, on the floor. "This town gives me the creeps though. Too much fresh air and drippy cheerfulness. Fools all of them. That will change soon enough. Where are the revised plans?"

LeFue adjusted his greasy ponytail and pulled out what looked like a big roll of graph paper from the pile on the desk.

"Here, this is where we are now. Here are the four orchards and the neighborhoods around them. The pipeline will go straight through there." He pointed at the paper. "Of course, these two neighborhoods will have to go. Eminent domain you know." He snickered. "The people can live here." He pointed to a small square on the edge of the town dump. "In their own, little housing project, where they belong. They don't know what's good for them. Imagine, taking up all that beautiful land to live there with their foolish houses and ridiculous families. Selfish. We will even get the town and the federal government to finance it after we pull out when they figure out they need amenities."

"Amenities?"

"Yes, roads, snow removal, water, electricity. The basics."

"Yes, silly fools. Look at them." Kettlebum turned towards the window. "They will never know what hit them. Is the plane ready? Is there enough tranquilizer? Remember, I want them agreeable, not passed out."

"Of course, they will be as compliant as lambs. Heh heh." He looked out the window, down at the crowd with sneer. "Like lambs to the slaughter."

"Looks like the local team lost. Perfect." He laughed. "After I deliver my speech, I will give you a nod to call the pilot."

"He'll fly out over the stadium and that plebeian rabble won't know what hit them," sneered LeFue. "So, what about the prize money?" he asked.

"What the lottery? That's a joke. Every ticket says me! Ha ha ha! The town council will be eating from my hands when I 'donate' it to the new town recreational center they are going to pay for. That money will stay where it is, in *my* bank account. Now let's get down there," Kettlebum clapped his hands together. "I smell bacon cooking. I am the judge of the barbecue, you know."

He walked over to the bar and squished his malodorous cigar into a huge glass ashtray. A spark flew down and landed on my tail. I could feel it smoldering in my fur. It took a good deal of control not to react. I swished my tail. I could smell the burnt hair. My discomfort built.

LeFue sniffed the air. "You should maybe cut down on those barbequed meats eh?"

"I'll barbeque you LeFue. Ha!" Kettlebum clapped him on the back and sent him sprawling through the door. I heard their voices get softer as they walked further away. A moment longer and I would be the barbeque.

I jumped up and ran to and fro.

"Yowwww! That smarts!"

The door opened and Ethan ran in.

"Are you alright, boy?" He patted my back and poured some water on my tail from a plastic water bottle in his knapsack.

"Brave old man! Very professional." He unsnapped the camera from my collar and held it up. "I think we have our evidence. "

I couldn't help but circling a few more times in glee, and pain.

"Okay, we are not done yet." He crept to the door and looked both ways before exiting into the hallway. "Come on Gus. We have some villains to expose."

CHAPTER EIGHT

THE TRUTH IS REVEALED

Ethan walked to the end of the hallway and entered another office. He zipped up his jacket, pulled off my café shirt and pulled a laptop out of his knapsack. "I just need to download our info onto a USB stick and get into the scoring office across the way."

He pulled up some footage onto the screen and saved it.

"Now comes the hard part. I hate public speaking but, well, someone has to do it. Let's go!"

Ethan and I walked quickly down the stairs and exited the building. We crossed the track and football field and made our way to the far bleachers next to the stage and scoreboard.

There were people everywhere enjoying the day. I had to dodge around their busy feet. The smell of food and happy voices filled the air. Football players and cheerleaders mingled in the crowd: mothers and kids, dads and uncles, policemen and teachers. The whole town was out. The air was filled with possibilities. Ethan picked up his cell and called Eva.

"Yes, we did it! I have it loaded onto the USB stick. Did the professor get on the plane? Yes! So far so good. I just hope I can get everyone's attention!"

We made our way up to the office and gave the USB stick to Ethan's friend Kenny.

"I hope you are right about this, man," said Kenny adjusting his glasses. "Just give me the signal and I will put this up on the big screen."

"Yeah dude. It's a total nightmare. But it won't be if we can tell the town the truth. Now is the perfect time. In ten minutes that is. Wait for me to touch my nose then play the file," replied Ethan.

"Got it! Good luck!"

They clapped hands and we were off again. Making our way to the podium.

Pinnnng! The microphone squealed loudly. A woman cleared her throat.

"And now, Mr. Englebert Kettlebum will announce the winners of the Best Ribs barbeque contest. Winner gets free barbeque from Mal's for a whole year, best fried pickles in the state. Mr. Kettlebum?"

Slowly, gloatingly, Kettlebum made his way to the microphone.

"Before I announce the winner, now that I have your attention, I just want to thank you all for being so kind to us." He leered at the town council sitting at a table below the stage. They had barbeque sauce on their faces. One was licking his fingers. "I would like to bring up my partner, Pierre LeFue. He has an important announcement to make about the progress of our orchard development. LeFue?"

Pierre LeFue slithered up to the podium. He flipped back his ponytail and smiled at the crowd. With a sneer, he pulled out a piece of paper and began reading about their plans to build a retirement community that the whole town would love.

Jacob O'Connor, Ethan's dad, stood up and raised his hand. "I live on the edge of the orchard. Will this affect my land at all?"

LeFue snickered, "Why not at all. No one will have to move, or do anything. It will be a great asset to the town. Wait until you see the amazing senior community we have planned. Leave it all up to us. You just have to sign over your deeds briefly to be reformatted. You know, just the local rights to the orchards, and all will go smooth as molasses." He winked at Kettlebum.

"Don't do it!" Ethan yelled from the crowd.

"What?" the crowd murmured.

"Don't listen to these guys. They are crooks!" Ethan ran up the stairs and made his way to the microphone. "They are planning on putting a pipeline through here and getting us all to pay for it. I have proof! He's going to drop tranquilizer from the sky to make everyone dizzy and open to suggestion but we neutralized it!"

"Get him outta here!" bellowed Kettlebum. His eyes blazed and his abdomen bulged. A button popped off his shirt.

LeFue sprang into action. He reached down to sweep Ethan's legs and tackle him but I was too quick for him. With incredible Westie speed, I flew up the stairs and launched myself at him. With teeth blazing, I grabbed ahold of his greasy ponytail. With a Velcro *Rippppp* it tore from his head. It was fake! Just like him. I ran around him in circles as he tried to get his hair back and grabbed his cell phone, which he dropped on the stage. There would be no signaling his buddies.

Ethan grabbed the microphone and pointed to his nose. "Now Kenny!"

All of a sudden, the huge widescreens on both sides of the bleachers sprang into life. In crystal clear sterio, LeFue and Kettlebum talked of their plans to drug the town and steal the land. They were caught!

"Don't listen to this, this kid! You can't prove a thing!" yelled Kettlebum and tried to get off the stage. "Planes? Tranquilizers? What nonsense!"

"Just look!" Ethan cried pointing at the sky.

In an instant the Doughton company plane flew overhead. It dipped and sped across the bleachers where the people were. People screamed and started to scatter.

"Don't worry! We neutralized it with the help of Professor Winter!" Ethan called into the microphone.

Like a downpour on a summer's day, purple soap suds descended from the plane onto the people below. The plane continued to fly back and forth, according to the villains' dastardly plan, until the whole field was covered in suds. Their evil desires were foiled however. The tranquilizer had been neutralized.

Kids from the town laughed and threw the innocuous suds at each other. They ran across the football field, kicking up bubbles and skidding through the grass. The scene looked like a crazy dance party without the techno music. A couple of grownups slipped. People of all ages smiled and spun around. Crisis averted.

"Hey that's the Doughton Industries plane. I worked on that last week," said Teddy Grafton, one of the town selectman.

Ethan still had the microphone. "They are trying to drug everyone so you all sign off on the agreements to let them have the land! They tried to drop drugs from their plane on the whole town. They are going to put a pipeline in and steal your land and all the neighboring houses! The town council already approved of Phase One. They just need the voter's signatures."

"Is this true?" Ethan's parents were in the front row. They turned and asked the town council. Tess popped her head out from behind Ethan's mom. The purple soap suds in her bright red hair made her look like a funny flower that had escaped from the garden.

The town council members fidgeted in their seats. They had pie on their faces and soap suds in their hair. The politicians looked embarrassed. They huffed and harrumphed but had no answers.

"We need an investigation! Lock these men up! They could have poisoned the whole town," said Ethan's dad.

"Why yes! Lock them up!" cried the town planner.

"Yes, lock them up!" called another councilman.

A lady councilman stood up and grabbed the microphone on the table.

"Where is the security?" she cried loudly. She adjusted her wig and brushed purple soap from her eyebrow most emphatically.

The police rushed to the stage. I bolted past LeFue and dropped his dripping ponytail at his feet. He reached down and stuck it back on but it was off to the right a bit too much. He looked a bit like an angry clown.

Clink. Sam Ruse the police chief rushed on stage and slapped the cuffs on LeFue. He spun around to face the crowd.

"You haven't seen the last of us!" screamed LeFue. "Fools!"

Kettlebum was led away in handcuffs, farting profusely as he passed. The grownups looked horrified but the kids thought it was pretty funny.

Ethan hugged is mom and dad who looked surprised, and relieved that we were okay. We were more than okay. We had saved the day!

Together, we made our way up to the orchard house to meet the professor. Past the Turkey Bowl, the town square, the church on the hill and through the orchards we walked. Ethan filled them in on our adventures as we went. Ethan's mom was a bit worried but looked pretty proud of her boy. Little Tess laughed and tossed an apple at me, although I was too fast for her efforts.

When we got to the professor's house, Eva and Professor W. came out to greet us. We all stood on the front lawn overlooking the orchard feeling pretty joyful.

"We did it!" shouted Eva giving Ethan and I a huge hug. Vader circled overhead calling gleefully. Ethan's drones spun and dipped overhead. I caught a glimpse of the naughty cat from Eva's house peeking out at us from some hedges on the edge of the property. Our parents shook hands with Professor W.

"So great to meet you. What an adventure these kids …*we all* have had! We are so grateful to you for helping," remarked Mr. O'Connor.

Ethan looked over at Eva and grinned. He looked relieved and psyched that we had pulled it off.

"So what's next, professor?" he asked.

Professor W. twirled his moustache and winked at the woodchuck staring at us through the window. He turned and looked out over acres of apple trees, golden and resplendent in the setting sun.

"Err, well, I have a few ideas! Cider anyone?"

CHAPTER NINE

NEW BEGINNINGS

If you walk up Witch Hill, which is steep and twisted all the way through, you will come to the top of an old apple orchard. It is very well cared for, full of life and loved as most beautiful things are. The town of Applewood has banded together, old and young, and rebuilt the fallen orchard. Apples gleam, delicious and full on branches old but less twisted and grateful to be bearing fruit. Don't worry about the two graveyards or the forest of the million eyes; the mansion in the middle has been converted to a beautiful cider house. The townsfolk visit there day and night and walk through the grounds admiring the view and the tasty cider that tickles the mouth and warms the spirit.

If you make your way back down Witch Hill and to the Westie Ranch, stop in and say hello. There is a family that lives there that loves the truth, and a scrappy white dog who is more than happy to bring it to you.

Join my mailing list for a free link to the audiobook of Westie Chronicles ch 1-4 and advanced notice on upcoming books in the series. Book two is in the works!

Go to:

www.WestieChronicles.com

If you enjoyed the story please leave a review on Amazon, if not please email me and let me know!!

Thanks for reading!!!!

Made in the USA
Middletown, DE
01 April 2017